Zadie's
Last Race

Martyn Hobbs

About this Book

For the Student

🎧 Listen to all of the story and do some activities on your Audio CD
💬 Talk about the story
beat• When you see the blue dot you can check the word in the glossary
 Prepare for Cambridge English: Key (KET) for Schools

For the Teacher

 A state-of-the-art interactive learning environment with 1000s of free online self-correcting activities for your chosen readers.

Go to our Readers Resource site for information on using readers and downloadable Resource Sheets, photocopiable Worksheets and Answer Keys. Plus free sample tracks from the story.

www.helblingreaders.com

For lots of great ideas on using Graded Readers consult Reading Matters, the Teacher's Guide to using Helbling Readers.

Level 3 Structures

Present continuous for future	Cardinal / ordinal numbers
Present perfect	One / ones
Present perfect versus past simple	Reflexive pronouns
Should / shouldn't (advice and obligation)	Indefinite pronouns
Must / should	
Need to / have to	Too plus adjective
Will	Not plus adjective plus enough
	Relative pronouns who, which and that
Ever / never	Prepositions of time, place and movement
Would like	
So do I / neither do I	
Question tags	

Structures from lower levels are also included.

NEW for Helbling Readers

Helbling Readers e-zone is the brand new state-of-the-art easy-to-use interactive learning environment from Helbling Languages. Each book has its own set of online interactive self-correcting cyber homework activities containing a range of reading comprehension, vocabulary, listening comprehension, grammar and exam preparation exercises.

Students test their language skills in a stimulating interactive environment. All activities can be attempted as many times as necessary and full results and feedback are given as soon as the deadline has been reached. Single student access is also available.

Teachers register free of charge to set up classes and assign individual and class homework sets. Results are provided automatically once the deadline has been reached and detailed reports on performance are available at a click.

1000s of free online interactive activities now available.

www.helbling-ezone.com

Contents

Before Reading   6
Zadie's Last Race   11
After Reading   54
Glossary   62

Before Reading

1 Look at the picture and answer the questions on pages 8 and 9.

Before Reading

Before Reading

1 Find these things in the picture on pages 6 and 7 and label them.

a) parked cars   b) headlights   c) beams
d) railings   e) streetlamp   f) kerb
g) tyre   h) driver   i) pavement

2 Imagine you are on the road in the picture. Discuss the following questions with your partner.

a) What can you see?
b) What can you smell?
c) What can you hear?

3 Look at the picture again, and at the front cover of the book. What do you think is going to happen? Make notes.

4 In groups, share your ideas from Exercise 3. Then write a description of what is happening in the picture and what happens next.

- Use as many of the words from Exercise 1 as you can.
- Use your ideas from Exercise 2 to add atmosphere.

5 Read your descriptions to the class and choose the best one.

Before Reading

6 Listen, look at the pictures, then write the names of each of the characters.

> Mr Bray   Grace   Holly   Charlie   Zadie   Jack

a) ....
b) ....
c) ....
d) ....
e) ....
f) ....

7 Can you guess? Look at the pictures in the book and answer the questions. Then exchange your ideas with the rest of the class.

a) When and where is the story set?
....

b) Why are Zadie and Holly running together?
....

c) What happens to Zadie after the accident?
....

d) Where is the strange world Zadie finds herself in?
....

9

Zadie's Last Race

³ This is what happened.
It was seven o'clock on a dark autumn evening. October was coming to an end and Halloween• and Guy Fawkes Night• were fast approaching. The air was cold and you could already see a touch of frost• on the parked cars. Most people were sitting comfortably at home having dinner or watching TV (or doing both at the same time). Others were out in their back gardens. These people couldn't wait for the last day of the month or the fifth of November. They were busy exploding bangers• or firing rockets• up into the night sky. The rockets screamed and burst into blue, red and green stars.
Two other people were out that evening.
They were jogging along the pavements under the yellow streetlamps. One of them was in front, running smoothly•. The other one was struggling• behind. And she wasn't very happy.

11

19:05

Holly stopped. She put her hands on her waist•, bent over, and started coughing•. Zadie heard her running partner and ran back to join her. 'Are you OK?' asked Zadie.

Holly looked up and tried to smile. It was difficult! She was gasping• for breath.

'Zadie, how come you're such a... (*cough, cough*)... such a great runner? I mean... (*cough, cough*)... I feel terrible. I'm so hot and tired. But look at you... (*cough, cough*)... you aren't even sweating•!'

'Well, you know me. I love running!' said Zadie with a big smile. She found smiling easy!

'It's no good. I can't go on,' said Holly.

Zadie's Last Race

'You can't stop yet!' said Zadie. 'We've only done a couple of kilometres. How are you going to win the marathon on Saturday?'
'I'm not going to win the marathon,' said Holly. 'You are.'
'No way•!' Zadie laughed.
She checked her watch.
'Come on, why don't we run for another half hour?'
'I'm sorry, Zadie, I can't. I've felt awful all day. I want to go home and get into a lovely hot bath.'
'Well, do you want me to jog back home with you?' asked Zadie.
Holly smiled guiltily•.
'I think I'll give my dad a call. He'll pick me up and give me a lift home.'
And with that, Holly pulled out her mobile.

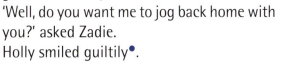

19:14

'There he is!' said Holly.
A big, shiny, dark-blue car approached and parked next to them at the side of the road. The electric window rolled• down.
'Hi, girls,' said Mr Wells.
'Hi Dad. Thanks for coming to get me.'
'That's all right,' Holly's father replied. 'It's a cold night for running. Would you like a lift home, too, Zadie?'
'No thanks,' said Zadie. 'I want to do a bit more running.'
'Well, don't leave it too late. It's already quarter past seven.'
'See you tomorrow, Zadie,' said Holly, getting into the passenger seat.
'Do you want to go for a run before school?' asked Zadie.
Holly laughed.
'No way!'
The car door slammed• shut, Holly's father gave a wave, and they drove away along the road. Zadie bent down and tied up her laces•. She looked both ways along the road.
For a moment she was undecided. She was only about 20 minutes from home, but that wasn't enough exercise. She decided to take the long route• home. And to run fast.
So Zadie got into the starting position for a 100 metre race. Then she said:
'Ready...
Steady...
Go!'
And she raced off towards the park.

Zadie's Last Race

`20:10`

Westbourne Park was quiet and empty under the starlit• sky. Even the fireworks were silent here. It seemed that everybody was in their homes except for one single girl. The only things Zadie could hear were the sound of her breathing, the beating of her heart, and the noise of her trainers on the hard pavement. She was running beside the park. And as she ran, she was counting the iron railings of the park fence.

'210... 220... 230...'

This was when she felt happiest. This was when she felt free.

She was running easily, she was running quickly. She was moving like a perfect machine, like an arrow• flying through the air...

She felt light and fit• and strong. She had no worries, no aches or pains. She wasn't thinking about school or homework or a silly argument she had with Jack that afternoon. In fact, she only had one thought in her head.

'240... 250... 260...'

She couldn't wait for the race. And she knew she could win.

Zadie was running towards the corner of the park. Then she had to cross the road, turn left, and head back towards the town centre. She was only about 10 minutes away from her house. Maybe she could run even faster!

Then behind her she heard an angry sound. It was the roar• of a car. The car was going fast – a lot faster than her – and it was coming in her direction.

This is how it started.

It was a morning near the beginning of the autumn term. It was the beginning of the worst time of the year. The summer holidays were over. The days were growing shorter and the nights were growing longer. All the light and joy and warmth of the world was disappearing and now there was nothing left to look forward to except the end of term and Christmas. Zadie met Holly on her way to school.

'Have you seen this?' asked Holly.

Holly held up her mobile. Zadie read:

Zadie's Last Race

'Hey, there's going to be a marathon here in Westbourne!' Zadie said excitedly.
She read more of the webpage.
'It's open to all ages!'
Zadie loved racing against other runners, no matter how old or how fast they were. She read to the bottom of the page.
'And it's raising money for the animal rescue centre!'
Zadie's dog Scamp, like Holly's dog Eco, both came from animal rescue centres. Zadie and Holly knew how important they were for saving animals and finding them homes.
'Wow, Holly! This is perfect!'
'So do you plan to do it, Zadie?'
'Are you kidding•? It'll be brilliant!' she said, smiling.

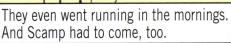

🎧 And so we come again to a morning towards the end of October. It was another normal morning at school.
Holly sneezed• all through the Chemistry lesson. Everybody looked at her, including Mr Bray, their red-faced teacher. People had different theories why he had such a red face. Some thought he was always hot. Some thought he was always embarrassed. Others thought it was because he made too many explosions in the laboratory.
'Are you all right, Holly?' he asked.
'I think these chemicals are making me sneeze,' she said.
'Well, stop sniffing• them!' said Jack.
Everybody laughed, except Mr Bray. His face went a bit redder.
'Keep your voice down, Jack,' he said.
At lunchtime Holly said, 'I think I'll miss the run today. I'm feeling a bit weird•.'
'No worries•,' said Zadie. 'But I'm still going to do it. I want to run against the clock•.'

22

Zadie's Last Race

So Zadie put on her tracksuit and trainers and set off round the school field.

Her first lap• was fast. Her second lap was faster. On her third lap she was running faster than ever. She was running past some bushes• at the furthest point from the school buildings when she heard terrifying cries. Four crazy creatures jumped out at her, howling• like wolves and waving huge coloured hands.

Zadie screamed. And the four monsters laughed.

Then she saw the monsters were wearing Halloween masks. And one of them was Jack.

'That was really stupid, Jack!' she shouted.

'Running is stupid,' said Jack.

'It wasn't funny!'

'Oh yes it was!' he said. 'You looked so scared!'

The four boys walked back across the field laughing loudly.

After school, Zadie called round for Holly (who said she felt a bit better) and they started jogging along the streets of Westbourne. But Holly didn't feel very well so Zadie carried on running on her own. And then...

This is what happened next.
Zadie was running towards the corner when behind her she heard the sound of a car. It was going fast – a lot faster than her – and it was getting closer. She slowed down and looked back over her shoulder. The street was empty apart from a few parked cars – but then she saw the headlights of a car speeding• in her direction. They burned brightly in the night like two angry eyes. She knew immediately that the car was going faster than the speed limit•.

So Zadie continued to the corner and then waited. There was time to cross the road – but it was better to wait. This car was in a hurry!

Zadie's Last Race

So she jogged on the spot• on the pavement, keeping warm, looking ahead, while the car roared like a monster behind her. She saw the beams• from its headlights sweep• from one side of the road to the other.
'That's weird,' she thought. 'Has the driver lost control?'
And then it all happened so quickly.
The car was coming closer and closer.
There was a loud crunch•.
Zadie began to turn her head.
There was a screaming and a roaring so close to her.
The car was just behind her.
And then her world changed forever.

25

Zadie was... somewhere.
She was lying on her back. She didn't know why. She couldn't remember anything.
She felt strange. She felt...
She didn't know what she felt. She wasn't in pain but... what was it? What was she feeling?
She didn't know. She had no words.
Then she heard a sound. It was the sound of a car engine. For a moment a wave of terror flowed through her. But this car wasn't moving. It was just the sound of a car engine standing by the side of the road. The sort of sound you hear every day.
And then there were voices. There were men's voices. They weren't talking to her, they were talking to each other. The men sounded scared.
'What have you done, Jack?'
'I didn't see her there!'

Zadie's Last Race

'But what happened?'
'The car skidded• or something. It went all over the place•.'
'Is she all right?'
'I dunno•, man.'
'Take a look.'
'I can't. I'm – I'm – worried, man. I can't do it.'
'Then I'll look.'
Boots scraped• on the road. A dark shape stood over her.
'What's happening, Charlie? Is she OK?'
'It's too dark. I can't see.'
'What are we going to do?'
'Let's get out of here!'
The men got back into the car.
There was a crunching noise, a screech• of tyres•, and the car drove off into the night.

Zadie breathed.
She breathed slowly, trying to think.
Was she all right? Was she going to be all right?
She couldn't tell.
And then...
And then she felt her body slowly rise up from the ground.
Was this really happening?
She thought her body lifted completely off the road.
Her feet were rising above her head.
Her head was pointing down to the ground.
And then...
And then a shower of stars started falling from the sky. There were hundreds of them. Thousands of them. There were a million stars all falling from the sky, slowly, silently, turning the night sky white.

Zadie's Last Race

The next morning a group of students was standing by the school gate. They were listening to Holly, and they couldn't believe their ears●. When she finished nobody said anything. They were all in shock●.
'So her legs are broken?' asked Ricky.
Holly nodded●.
'Is she talking?' asked Grace.
'Not yet. She hasn't woken up. She's still unconscious●.'
They all thought about that.
'Who did it?' asked Jack.
'We don't know. The police found the car this morning by the river. Its front was smashed in.'
'Can we visit her?' asked David.
'Well, her parents are going to be with her all today. But maybe tomorrow.'
They couldn't concentrate during their lessons. They couldn't think about anything except Zadie. And so they waited and waited and the hours passed so slowly.

29

Zadie's Last Race

🎧 They sat down around the bed and looked at Zadie. She had plaster• on both her broken legs, and there were a few scratches• and bruises• on her arms, but her head and face looked the same.
'We haven't left her side,' said Mrs Lewis. 'I was here with her dad all last night. And her brother Eric came in at lunchtime. I'm going to stay until about eight, then her dad will be back and take my place.'
'She looks very peaceful•,' said David.
'Yes, she does. She just seems to be sleeping soundly•. But it's so strange. Zadie never wants to go to bed. And she's always the first one to get up in the morning. She always wants to be up and skateboarding or playing football or running...'
'I know,' said Holly. 'Zadie's always so full of energy.'
The door opened. It was the nurse.
'Do you mind if your friends come in now?'

32

Zadie's Last Race

In the corridor outside the room, David and Holly spoke with the nurse.
'How long will she be unconscious?' asked David.
'We can't say for sure,' the nurse replied. 'We hope she'll make a full recovery•, but it's still early days. There's no sign of any brain damage•, and that's very good.'
'But she'll definitely wake up?' said Holly. 'I mean, she won't stay like that forever?'
'We hope she'll wake up soon,' said the nurse.
Holly suddenly felt weak and empty. Hope? <u>Hope</u>? That wasn't good enough. Zadie had to get better. She had to!
'Is there anything we can do?' asked David.
'If you come to visit Zadie, and talk to her, that will help. I'm sure of that. She's unconscious, but she may be able to hear you.'

Everything is white.
There is a fog•. There is a thick white fog. At least it seems to be fog, but there is no smell of fog. There is no taste of fog. And the air is neither hot nor cold, damp• nor dry. It is... nothing.
There are no sounds. There is no sense of direction.
The girl starts walking.
She stops.
She starts walking again.
Is she walking in the same direction?
Is she walking in a different direction?
Is she even walking?
She is moving her legs, she is sure of that. Her feet are moving, she can see them. But is she going anywhere?

Zadie's Last Race

She feels dizzy•. She feels sick. Her head is spinning•. 'I'm going to fall,' she thinks. But fall where? Where is down? Where is up? And who is 'she'?
'Who am I?' she asks herself.
There is no reply.
She repeats the question.
'Who am I?'
Her mouth shapes the words, she feels her lips move, her tongue move. She feels the air in her mouth. But there is no sound, no answer. She's scared now. Very scared.
'What is happening?' she asks herself.
There is no answer.
She wants to cry. There is a pressure behind her eyes.

And then two things happen.

She feels hot tears force themselves from the corner of her eyes and run down her face. They are hot and wet. They are real!

And she hears something. But what she hears terrifies her. The sound doesn't come from her. It isn't a sound she made. The sound comes from behind her.

It is like the sound of an autumn night. It is like the whisper of fallen leaves. It is the sound of autumn leaves moving on the pavement in the dark at night.

And then, with that strange whispering sound, there comes a smell. It is a damp smell, an earthy smell. It is the breath of an autumn garden at night. It is the smell of the damp earth and wet leaves. It is the smell of decay•, of things dying and falling apart. It is the smell of death.

Zadie's Last Race

She feels the air grow colder. And she sees the light change. It is growing dimmer•, greyer. What is causing that?

Then she sees why. A damp grey cloud is creeping• through the air and moving all around her. Suddenly she feels like ice. And she hears, or at least she thinks she hears, a low voice. It's a cold voice, a damp low voice, beside her. It is whispering in her ear – no!

It's whispering inside her head!

And the voice is repeating a word, the same word, and she knows immediately it is <u>her</u> name. It is saying: 'Zadie.'

That was her. She is Zadie!

And she knows she has to get away from this voice.

She has to escape.

She has to run!

After their visit was over, the friends went to a café. Nobody felt thirsty or hungry but they had to buy something, so Grace got them some milkshakes. She put the tray on the table and sat down. Nobody touched the drinks. They were all still in shock.

Then Holly started talking.

'It's good for us to talk to Zadie. That way we can try to stimulate her mind. We have to help her wake up.'

Now they had something positive to talk about, the friends started talking and making plans. After half an hour all their glasses were empty.

So they took it in turns* to visit Zadie in her hospital room.

Holly and Grace went on the first day and chatted about pets and dogs and boys. But after half an hour they ran out of* things to say and they just sat there, looking sadly at Zadie.

Ricky and Jack went the day after. Ricky sat close to the bed but Jack sat further away. He felt bad. He knew the last time he spoke to Zadie was by the school field. His gang scared her and made fun of her and laughed at her.

After that, David went on his own. He took his books with him and read to her. But he didn't read other people's books. He read his own stories. He knew Zadie enjoyed thrillers* so he read all his stories about David Delgado, the great detective. And when he finished those he started the adventures of the Black Corsair.

While he was reading he often looked up, hoping for signs of recovery*.

Zadie's Last Race

Zadie is running through a white world, a world of fog. She runs for minutes, she runs for hours. She can't tell how long she runs. But she runs until her legs are aching and her chest is burning and she has to stop.
She bends over and coughs and gasps for air. And while she is doing this, she remembers another person, another girl, coughing and tired and needing to rest. Who was that? Where did Zadie see her? Somehow she knows this girl was a friend.
What is her name?
Holly.
And as Zadie remembers the name she sees shapes come out of the fog. They are high and straight and much taller than her. They are houses.
And then she remembers another word.
Westbourne.
It is the town where she lives.

Zadie's Last Race

She sees trees growing in the air. She sees roads stretching out before her. She looks down and sees the kerbs• and the gutters• and the fallen leaves. She looks up and sees clouds moving slowly across the sky.
But her world is silent.
There are no dogs barking, no birds singing, no people talking. She gradually• understands that she is the only living creature in Westbourne.
Where is everybody?
She is all alone, except...
She hears a noise. It is a creak•, like the creak of a wooden floor.
Then she sees a shadow move across the pavement. It is a dark, shapeless shadow. The air grows colder and the light drains• from the sky. And a voice says:
'Zadie.'
She starts running.

The head races after her.

The road gets narrower and narrower.

It becomes a long, long corridor.

Zadie has no choice. She has to jump!

Holly and David were walking to school on a miserable wet morning. It was cold and raining but they didn't notice the weather. They were deep in conversation•. Of course, there was only one thing to talk about.

'The police have arrested• two guys,' said David. 'They think they were driving the car, but they aren't sure. There weren't any witnesses•.'

'This is all awful, awful, awful. I can't believe this has happened to Zadie.'

'Me neither. It seems unreal•. You know, I'm not doing any work at the moment,' said David.

'How can we?' asked Holly. 'How can we think or do anything while Zadie is in hospital?'

She stopped and looked closely at David.

'Do you think Zadie will ever wake up?'

'I don't know,' said David. 'But we can't give up hoping. We can't.'

Holly tried to sound upbeat•.

'Grace and I have had an idea,' she said. 'I hope it'll work.'

Zadie's Last Race

Grace put her MP3 player in its dock•.
'Turn up the volume,' said Holly.
'Sure,' said Grace. She pressed the button to get maximum volume, then turned to Zadie.
'We thought you might like to hear some music. We're going to play you some of our songs. You know, the Garage Girls. You really are the best drummer in the world, Zadie, and we want you to come back and play in our band.'
Holly wanted to say something but she felt too upset. So she just nodded at Grace and Grace pressed 'play'.
Loud music exploded into the room.
The door opened and a nurse poked• her head in. She was wondering what the noise was. But when she saw the two friends she quietly closed the door again. Holly and Grace didn't even see her. They were watching their drummer, searching for a reaction.

Zadie looks around her, amazed. The window has disappeared. And... she's not sure, but she thinks... she thinks she can hear voices.
They are distant and faint, but they are calling to her, calling across the emptiness. She has to get to them. She has to get home.
And then she finds herself in a road.
She knows this road. She recognises the trees and the parked cars and the houses on either side. And she knows that at the end of the road, near the corner, is a house with a blue front door and lights shining from the front room window. She knows her family is inside – her mother and father, her brother Eric and kid sister, Tania. They are inside the house and are waiting. They are waiting for her.

Zadie's Last Race

But something is wrong.
This road is like her road but... but something has changed. What is it? And then she realises with a chill• that there are iron railings in front of the houses. She remembers these railings from a different place. But where does she know them from?
Then in her mind she hears a voice.
'100... 90... 80... 70... 60...'
Where is the voice coming from? Why is it counting?
'50... 40... 30... 20...'
And then she hears a noise.
It is like the roar of a wild animal. It is like the roar of a hungry beast. It is the roar of a car and it is speeding towards her. Its headlights sway• from side to side.
The car is out of control.
And it is coming to get her.

🎧 Zadie looks up through the water. She is so short of breath•. Her lungs• are hurting. She doesn't have enough air...
Behind her, just behind her, there is a darkness. And this darkness is stretching out its long, thin arms. Its long, thin hands are trying to grab her. To hold on to her. To drag• her down to the ocean floor.
She looks up one last time and sees a light shape floating on the water. It is a boat!
It is her only hope. She has to reach it. Her hands are nearly touching it. If only she can get to the surface...
And then...
Her head rises above the water and she is swallowing• air in brilliant sunlight.
Strong arms reach down from the boat and pull her out of the water. She is safe!

Zadie's Last Race

'The sun rose over the island and poured its golden light over the sea. The light moved across the water, making the dark shadows disappear. The Black Corsair rubbed his eyes and looked up. He let his cloak fall to the bottom of his boat and felt the warmth of the sun on his arms...'

Something moved.

David saw it out of the corner of his eye. What was it? He looked up from his book. Everything seemed just the same: the lights on the machines, the bright tubes, the shiny wires. Zadie's head was in the same position on the pillow•. Her face was...

David couldn't believe his eyes. He leaned towards her. Was that a flicker• of movement? Was there movement around her eyes?

'Zadie,' he said. 'Zadie, are you there? Can you hear me? Can you open your eyes?'

He held his breath.

And Sleeping Beauty woke up.

This is how it ended.
Later that day Zadie spoke to a police officer and told him everything she could remember. It wasn't very much. She couldn't understand why, but when she thought of the accident, she always thought of her friend Jack.
Then she heard a voice in her head.
'What have you done, Jack?'
And then another.
'What's happening, Charlie?'
They were the names of the guys in the car, the guys who knocked her down●! She gave their names to the police. It was exactly what the police wanted to hear.
Then a doctor came in and talked to her. "Your legs need time to heal●, but you will be OK, and you'll make a full recovery," he said.
'Will I be able to run?' she asked nervously.
'Yes, you will,' said the doctor.
'So I'll run again,' she said happily to herself. 'I'll race again.'
Then Zadie thought of her last race, a race of life and death.
'I won that,' she thought. 'But it's a race I never want to run again.'

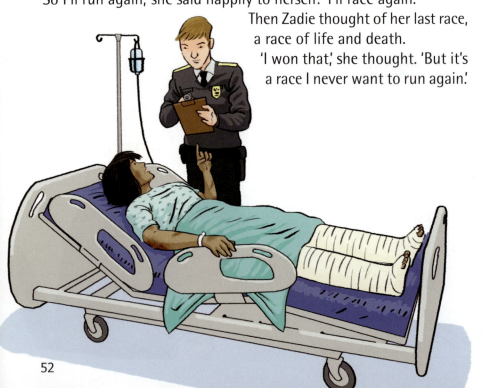

Zadie's Last Race

It was early on Monday morning. There was over half an hour before the first lesson but a crowd of students was already inside the school gates. They were chatting, talking quietly, waiting.
Then Jack, who was standing at the gates, turned to them and put his finger to his lips. They all fell silent.
They heard a car approach and stop outside. Car doors opened and closed. Then after a couple of minutes, a girl walked through the gates. She was walking with crutches• – but she was walking!
And then the whole crowd cheered and shouted out her name.
'Zadie! Zadie! Zadie! Zadie!'
Zadie looked at them all – she saw Grace and Ricky and Holly and Jack and David – and she smiled.
It was great to be back.

After Reading

Understanding the story

1 Who says these things? Write the names beside the speech bubbles.

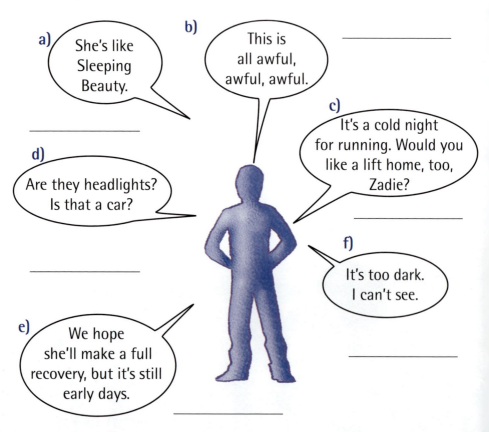

2 Now put the sentences above in the correct order of the story.

1	2	3	4	5	6

After Reading

3 Read the sentences and tick (✓) true (T) or false (F).

	T	F
a) Holly's father gave Zadie a lift home.	☐	☐
b) Zadie was running past Westbourne Park when she heard the car.	☐	☐
c) Charlie drove the car that knocked Zadie down.	☐	☐
d) On their first visit to the hospital, Holly and Grace played the Garage Girls' music.	☐	☐
e) A terrifying pumpkin mask chased Zadie down a long road.	☐	☐
f) David was reading a David Delgado story when Zadie woke up.	☐	☐

4 Imagine you are Zadie in the strange white world. You find a pen and a sheet of paper. Complete your message below. Say:

- what happened in Westbourne
- where you think you are
- what you can see / hear / smell
- what you are going to do next

5 Read out your messages in class. Choose the best messages.

After Reading

Vocabulary

1 Combine words from the two groups to make common expressions.

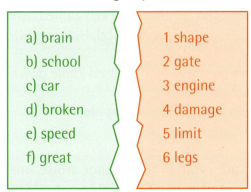

a) brain
b) school
c) car
d) broken
e) speed
f) great

1 shape
2 gate
3 engine
4 damage
5 limit
6 legs

2 Complete the sentences with expressions from Exercise 1.

a) First Zadie heard a .... and then she saw its headlights. The car was going faster than the ....
b) 'I saw Zadie in hospital. She hasn't got .... but she's got two .... !
c) All Zadie's school mates were waiting at the .... They thought she looked in ....

3 When can you use these phrases? Match.

a) ☐ No way!
b) ☐ Are you kidding?
c) ☐ I guess so.
d) ☐ No worries.
e) ☐ That's weird.
f) ☐ Sure.

1 You think something is OK.
2 You think something is strange.
3 You want to say 'yes'.
4 You want to say a definite 'no'.
5 You think somebody is joking.
6 You more or less agree with somebody.

After Reading

4 Complete the speech bubbles with the correct verbs.

scraped   crunched   screamed   whispered   howled

a) Rockets .... in the sky.

b) Jack was wearing a mask and he .... like a wolf.

c) Two men walked towards ...e and their boots .... on the pavement.

d) A voice .... quietly in my ear.

e) I was running away and the car .... against the kerb.

5 Match the beginnings and ends of the sentences.

a) ☐ She was moving like   1 the whisper of fallen leaves.
b) ☐ The headlights burned like   2 the roar of a hungry beast.
c) ☐ The car makes a noise like   3 two angry eyes.
d) ☐ She hears something like   4 a perfect machine.

6 Now write more sentences. Imagine Zadie experienced these things in the strange white world.

a) The fog is thick like...
b) The buildings are like...
c) The creature is like...
d) She feels cold like...

After Reading

Grammar

Practise the Present Perfect and Past Simple

1 Write the questions and short answers.

   a) Zadie / win / a race? (✓)
   <u>Has Zadie ever won a race? Yes, she has.</u>
   b) Ricky / go / to America? (✘)
   ....
   c) Grace, Holly and Zadie / play / a concert? (✓)
   ....
   d) David / write / a story? (✓)
   ....
   e) Holly / live / in a tree house? (✓)
   ....
   f) Jack / get / full marks in a test? (✘)
   ....

2 Give more information to the answers in Exercise 1. Complete the sentences with the Past Simple. Then match them with the questions above.

   a) They .... (give) a concert at Westbourne School in December. ☐
   b) He .... (write) his latest story last weekend. ☐
   c) She .... (stay) in the tree at the end of her garden for weeks. ☐
   d) She .... (finish) three minutes ahead of the girl who came second. ☐
   e) But a year ago he .... (meet) Holly's American cousin. ☐
   f) In fact, he .... (fall) asleep during his last test! ☐

After Reading

Practise will

3 Fill in the gaps with *will/won't* and the verbs below.

> hear   drive   run   see   do   win   read   relax

a) **Zadie:** .... you .... in the marathon with me, Holly?
   Holly: Well, OK, if you want. But I .... !
b) **Charlie:** What should we do now?
   Jack: I think I .... the car down to the river.
c) **Zadie:** Oh no! There's the monster! I can hide behind that building. Then it .... me.
d) **Ricky:** How can we help Zadie wake up?
   David: I think I .... her some of my stories. And I hope she .... them.
e) **Grace:** What .... you .... next, Zadie?
   Zadie: I'm not sure. I think I .... at home. But you know that's difficult for me!

Practise question tags

4 The police asked Zadie lots of questions when she woke up in the hospital. Complete their questions with the correct question tag.

a) You're well enough to talk, *aren't you*?
b) You've had a terrible experience, ... ?
c) Holly planned to run in the marathon with you, ... ?
d) Jack and Charlie were the men in the car, ... ?
e) Your mother is waiting outside the room, ... ?
f) Your friends will be happy to see you, ... ?

59

After Reading
Test

 1 **Listen to the conversations and choose the correct picture to answer each question.**

a) Which festival is very near when the story begins?

1 ☐ 2 ☐ 3 ☐

b) What was Zadie counting while she was running?

1 ☐ 2 ☐ 3 ☐

c) Why did Holly want Zadie to run in the marathon?

1 ☐  2 ☐  3 ☐

d) What name did Zadie remember when she spoke to the policeman?

1 ☐  2 ☐  3 ☐

After Reading

K 2 Read the sentences about the story and choose the best word or words (1, 2 or 3) to finish each one.

a) Zadie and Holly were planning to run in…
   1 a school marathon.   2 a charity fun run.
   3 an important race.

b) When Zadie was running in the school field, Jack and his friends…
   1 frightened her.   2 chased her.
   3 shouted at her.

c) After the accident, Zadie felt that she was…
   1 falling through space.   2 sinking into the sea.
   3 floating above the ground.

d) After their visit to the hospital, the friends discussed their plans
   1 in the park.   2 at Holly's house.
   3 in a café.

e) When Zadie was in the white world, she heard her name and she…
   1 started running.   2 tried to hide.
   3 started crying.

f) To help Zadie wake up, Holly and Grace decided to…
   1 tell jokes.   2 play their music.
   3 sing their songs.

g) Zadie woke up while David was reading a story about…
   1 the Black Corsair.   2 the Great Detective.
   3 the Garage Girls.

3 Look at the pictures on pages 52 and 53 in the story. Ask and answer questions about them.

- Who can you see in the pictures?
- What is happening?
- What is Zadie saying to the policeman?

61

Glossary

11 **bangers:** fireworks that explode with a bang
frost: ice
Guy Fawkes Night: 5th November, when a figure (guy) is burnt on a bonfire and fireworks are set off
Halloween: 31st October, when children dress up in costumes and go from house to house 'trick or treating'
rockets:

smoothly: (here) without problems
struggling: finding (here) it difficult to run

12 **coughing:** making a noise as you force air out of your mouth
gasping: taking air in quickly through your mouth
sweating: when liquid comes out of your skin because you are hot
waist: middle part of your body

13 **guiltily:** feeling bad because she knows she is doing something wrong
no way: definitely not

14 **laces:** cords to fasten shoes
rolled: moved smoothly
route: way
slammed: closed with force

17 **arrow:**
fit: healthy
roar: noise a lion makes
starlit: filled with stars

19 **kidding:** joking

22 **no worries:** don't worry; no problem
run against the clock: run measuring how long it takes
sneezed: when air comes out of your nose and mouth in an uncontrolled way with a loud noise
sniffing: smelling
weird: strange

23 **bushes:** small trees
howling: making the loud cry that wolves make
lap: circuit; once around the track

Glossary

24 **speeding:** going very fast
speed limit: maximum speed cars should travel at on a road
25 **beams:** lines of light
crunch: sound of something breaking
on the spot: in one place
sweep: move quickly and smoothly
27 **all over the place:** in every direction
dunno: don't know
scraped: scratched with an unpleasant noise
screech: loud, high noise
skidded: went out of control
tyres: rubber parts of wheels
29 **believe their ears:** believe what they were hearing
nodded: moved her head up and down
unconscious: not awake
were in shock: were completely shocked
31 **motionless:** not moving
32 **bruises:** dark marks on the skin
peaceful: quiet and calm
plaster: hard white material that covers and protects broken bones
scratches: marks where the skin is cut
soundly: deeply
33 **brain damage:** injury to the brain
make a full recovery: get completely better
34 **damp:** wet
fog:

35 **dizzy:** feeling that you can't balance
spinning: turning round and round
36 **decay:** when something dies and falls to pieces
37 **creeping:** moving slowly
dimmer: less bright
38 **ran out of:** had no more left
signs of recovery: something that shows she will get better
thrillers: exciting mystery stories
took it in turns: did something one after the other

63

41 **creak:** a long low sound
   drains: pours away
   gradually: slowly
   gutters: edges of the road where water flows away
   kerbs: edges of the pavement
44 **arrested:** taken to the police station to ask about a crime
   deep in conversation: concentrating on talking
   unreal: not true; impossible
   upbeat: cheerful and hopeful
   witnesses: people who saw what happened
45 **dock:** piece of equipment in which you put an MP3 player to play it through speakers
   poked: quickly put
46 **faint:** (here) not very loud
   kid sister: younger sister
47 **chill:** cold feeling
   sway: move from side to side
49 **plunging:** diving
   sinking: falling in water
50 **drag:** pull
   lungs: organs humans breathe with
   short of breath: having no breath
   swallowing: (here) breathing in air
51 **flicker:** very small amount
   pillow: cushion in a bed
52 **heal:** become well again
   knocked her down: hit her with the car
53 **crutches:**